SIMON & SCHUSTER BOOKS FOR YOUNG READERS
An imprint of Simon & Schuster Children's Publishing Division
1230 Avenue of the Americas, New York, New York 10020

For information about special discounts for bulk purchases, please
contact Simon & Schuster Special Sales at 1-866-506-1949 or
business@simonandschuster.com.
The Simon & Schuster Speakers Bureau can bring authors to your live
event. For more information or to book an event, contact the
Simon & Schuster Speakers Bureau at 1-866-248-3049 or visit our
website at www.simonspeakers.com.
Manufactured in China 0119 MCM
33 35 34
ISBN: 978-0-671-50118-1

A TREASURY OF MOTHER GOOSE

ILLUSTRATED BY HILDA OFFEN

Simon & Schuster Books for Young Readers

Contents

Index of First Lines, page 154

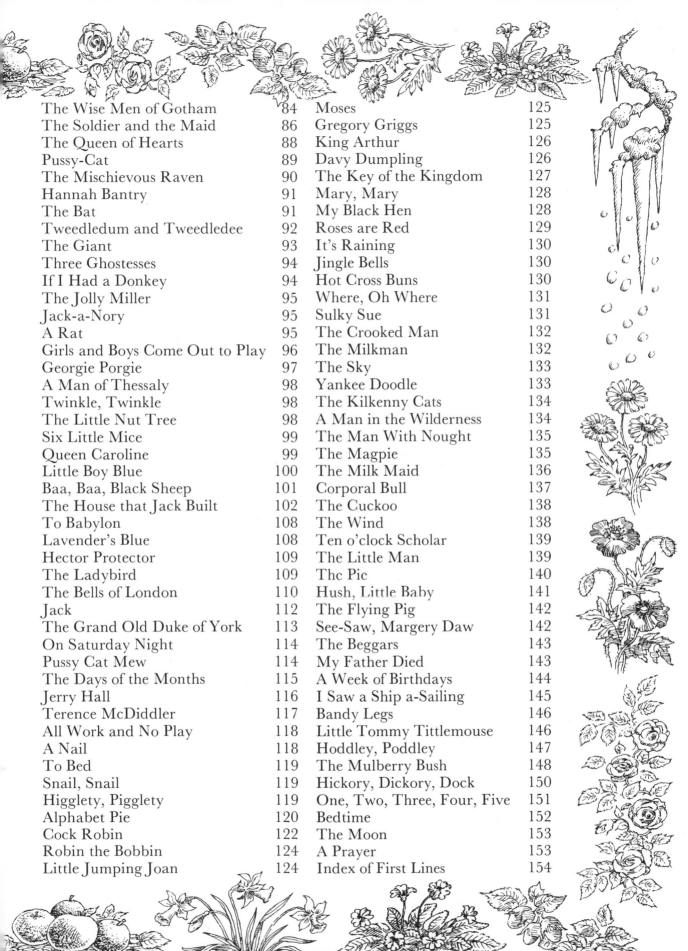

OLD MOTHER GOOSE

Old Mother Goose,
When she wanted to wander,
Would ride through the air
On a very fine gander.

Mother Goose had a house,
'Twas built in a wood,
Where an owl at the door
For sentinel stood.

She had a son Jack,
A plain-looking lad,
He was not very good,
Nor yet very bad.

She sent him to market,
A live goose he bought;
See, mother, says he,
I have not been for nought.

Jack's goose and her gander
Grew very fond;
They'd both eat together,
Or swim in the pond.

Jack found one fine morning,
As I have been told,
His goose had laid him
An egg of pure gold.

Jack ran to his mother
The news for to tell,
She called him a good boy,
And said it was well.

Jack sold his gold egg
To a merchant untrue,
Who cheated him out of
A half of his due.

Then Jack went a-courting
A lady so gay,
As fair as the lily,
And sweet as the May.

The merchant and squire
Soon came at his back
And began to belabor
The sides of poor Jack.

Then old Mother Goose
That instant came in,
And turned her son Jack
Into famed Harlequin.

JACK AND JILL

Jack and Jill
Went up the hill,
To fetch a pail of water;
Jack fell down,
And broke his crown,
And Jill came tumbling after.

Then up Jack got,
And home did trot,
As fast as he could caper;
Went to bed,
To mend his head
With vinegar and brown paper.

When Jill came in,
How she did grin
To see Jack's paper plaster;
His mother, vexed,
Did whip her next,
For laughing at Jack's disaster.

Now Jack did laugh
And Jill did cry,
But her tears did soon abate;
Then Jill did say,
That they should play
At see-saw across the gate.

SIMPLE SIMON

Simple Simon met a pieman,
Going to the fair;
Says Simple Simon to the pieman,
Let me taste your ware.

Says the pieman to Simple Simon,
Show me first your penny;
Says Simple Simon to the pieman,
Indeed I have not any.

14

Simple Simon went a-fishing,
For to catch a whale;
All the water he had got
Was in his mother's pail.

Simple Simon went to look
If plums grew on a thistle;
He pricked his fingers very much,
Which made poor Simon whistle.

He went for water in a sieve
But soon it all ran through;
And now poor Simple Simon
Bids you all adieu.

MARY'S LAMB

Mary had a little lamb,
Its fleece was white as snow;
And everywhere that Mary went
The lamb was sure to go.

It followed her to school one day,
That was against the rule;
It made the children laugh and play
To see a lamb at school.

And so the teacher turned it out,
But still it lingered near,
And waited patiently about
Till Mary did appear.

Why does the lamb love Mary so?
The eager children cry;
Why, Mary loves the lamb, you know,
The teacher did reply.

ONE, TWO

1, 2,
Buckle my shoe;

3, 4,
Knock at the door;

5, 6,
Pick up sticks;

7, 8,
Lay them straight;

9, 10,
A big fat hen;

11, 12,
Dig and delve;

13, 14,
Maids a-courting;

15, 16,
Maids in the kitchen;

17, 18,
Maids a-waiting;

19, 20,
My plate's empty.

THE PUMPKIN EATER

Peter, Peter, pumpkin eater,
Had a wife and couldn't keep her;
He put her in a pumpkin shell,
And there he kept her very well.

JACK SPRAT

Jack Sprat could eat no fat,
His wife could eat no lean,
And so between them both, you see,
They licked the platter clean.

DOCTOR FOSTER

Doctor Foster went to Gloucester
In a shower of rain;
He stepped in a puddle,
Right up to his middle,
And never went there again.

THE OWL

A wise old owl sat in an oak,
The more he heard the less he spoke;
The less he spoke the more he heard.
Why aren't we all like that wise old bird?

RING-A-RING O'ROSES

Ring-a-ring o' roses,
A pocket full of posies,
A-tishoo! A-tishoo!
We all fall down.

DING, DONG, BELL

Ding, dong, bell,
Pussy's in the well.
Who put her in?
Little Johnny Green.
Who pulled her out?
Little Tommy Stout.
What a naughty boy was that
To try to drown poor pussy cat,
Who never did him any harm,
But killed the mice in his father's barn.

WHAT CAN THE MATTER BE?

O dear, what can the matter be?
Dear, dear, what can the matter be?
O dear, what can the matter be?
Johnny's so long at the fair.

He promised he'd buy me a fairing to please me,
And then for a kiss, oh! he vowed he would tease me,
He promised he'd bring me a bunch of blue ribbons
To tie up my bonny brown hair.

And it's O dear, what can the matter be?
Dear, dear, what can the matter be?
O dear, what can the matter be?
Johnny's so long at the fair.

He promised to buy me a pair of sleeve buttons,
A pair of new garters that cost him but twopence,
He promised he'd bring me a bunch of blue ribbons
To tie up my bonny brown hair.

And it's O dear, what can the matter be?
Dear, dear, what can the matter be?
O dear, what can the matter be?
Johnny's so long at the fair.

He promised he'd bring me a basket of posies,
A garland of lilies, a garland of roses,
A little straw hat, to set off the blue ribbons
That tie up my bonny brown hair.

THE LION AND THE UNICORN

The lion and the unicorn
Were fighting for the crown;
The lion beat the unicorn
All around the town.

Some gave them white bread,
And some gave them brown;
Some gave them plum cake
And sent them out of town.

TO MARKET

To market, to market, to buy a fat pig,
Home again, home again, jiggety-jig;

To market, to market, to buy a fat hog,
Home again, home again, jiggety-jog.

BOBBY SHAFTOE

Bobby Shaftoe's gone to sea,
Silver buckles on his knee;
He'll come back and marry me,
Bonny Bobby Shaftoe.

Bobby Shaftoe's fat and fair,
Combing down his yellow hair,
He's my love for evermair,
Bonny Bobby Shaftoe.

OLD KING COLE

Old King Cole was a merry old soul,
And a merry old soul was he;
He called for his pipe and he called for his bowl,
And he called for his fiddlers three.

Every fiddler he had a fiddle,
And a very fine fiddle had he;
Oh, there's none so rare as can compare
With King Cole and his fiddlers three.

WILLIE WINKIE

Wee Willie Winkie runs through the town,
Upstairs and downstairs in his nightgown,
Rapping at the window, crying through the lock,
Are all the children in their beds, it's past eight o'clock?

DAPPLE GRAY

I had a little pony,
His name was Dapple Gray;
I lent him to a lady
To ride a mile away.
She whipped him, she slashed him,
She rode him through the mire;
I would not lend my pony now,
For all the lady's hire.

PAT-A-CAKE

Pat-a-cake, pat-a-cake, baker's man,
Bake me a cake as fast as you can;
Pat it and prick it, and mark it with T,
Put it in the oven for Tommy and me.

LITTLE MISS MUFFET

Little Miss Muffet sat on a tuffet,
Eating her curds and whey;
There came a big spider, who sat down beside her
And frightened Miss Muffet away.

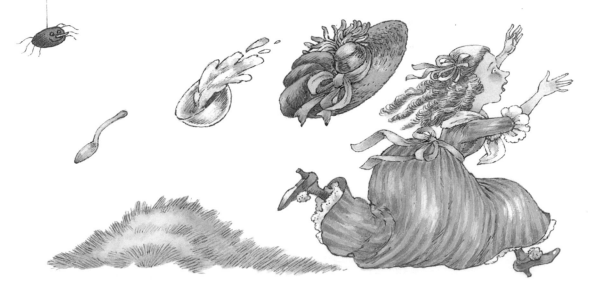

THREE MEN IN A TUB

Rub-a-dub-dub,
Three men in a tub,
And how do you think they got there?
The butcher, the baker,
The candlestick-maker,
They all jumped out of a rotten potato.
'Twas enough to make a man stare.

ONE MISTY, MOISTY MORNING

One misty, moisty morning,
When cloudy was the weather,
I chanced to meet an old man
Clothed all in leather.

He began to compliment,
And I began to grin,
How do you do, and how do you do,
And how do you do again?

POLLY FLINDERS

Little Polly Flinders
Sat amongst the cinders,
Warming her pretty little toes;
Her mother came and caught her,
And whipped her little daughter
For spoiling her nice new clothes.

HUSH-A-BYE

Hush-a-bye, baby, on the tree top,
When the wind blows, the cradle will rock;
When the bough breaks, the cradle will fall;
Down will come baby, cradle and all.

THE NORTH WIND

The north wind doth blow,
And we shall have snow,
And what will poor Robin do then,
    Poor thing?
He'll sit in a barn,
And keep himself warm,
And hide his head under his wing,
    Poor thing.

OLD MOTHER HUBBARD

Old Mother Hubbard
Went to the cupboard,
To fetch her poor dog a bone;
But when she got there
The cupboard was bare
And so the poor dog had none.

She went to the baker's
To buy him some bread;
But when she came back
The poor dog was dead.

She went to the joiner's
To buy him a coffin;
But when she came back
The poor dog was laughing.

She took a clean dish
To get him some tripe;
But when she came back
He was smoking a pipe.

She went to the fishmonger's
To buy him some fish;
But when she came back
He was licking the dish.

She went to the tavern
For white wine and red;
But when she came back
The dog stood on his head.

She went to the fruiterer's
To buy him some fruit;
But when she came back
He was playing the flute.

She went to the tailor's
To buy him a coat;
But when she came back
He was riding a goat.

She went to the hatter's
To buy him a hat;
But when she came back
He was feeding the cat.

She went to the barber's
To buy him a wig;
But when she came back
He was dancing a jig.

She went to the cobbler's
To buy him some shoes;
But when she came back
He was reading the news.

She went to the seamstress
To buy him some linen;
But when she came back
The dog was a-spinning.

She went to the hosier's
To buy him some hose;
But when she came back
He was dressed in his clothes.

The dame made a curtsey,
The dog made a bow;
The dame said, "Your servant,"
The dog said, "Bow-wow."

LITTLE BO-PEEP

Little Bo-peep has lost her sheep,
And can't tell where to find them;
Leave them alone, and they'll come home,
Bringing their tails behind them.

Little Bo-peep fell fast asleep,
And dreamed she heard them bleating;
But when she awoke, she found it a joke,
For they were still a-fleeting.

Then up she took her little crook,
Determined for to find them;
She found them indeed, but it made her heart bleed
For they'd left their tails behind them.

It happened one day, as Bo-peep did stray
Into a meadow hard by,
There she espied their tails side by side,
All hung on a tree to dry.

She heaved a sigh, and wiped her eye,
And over the hillocks went rambling,
And tried what she could as a shepherdess should,
To tack each again to its lambkin.

MY MOTHER SAID

My mother said, I never should
Play with the gypsies in the wood.
If I did, then she would say:
Naughty girl to disobey.
Your hair shan't curl and your shoes shan't shine,
You gypsy girl you shan't be mine.
And my father said that if I did,
He'd rap my head with the teapot lid.

COCK A DOODLE DOO

Cock a doodle doo!
My dame has lost her shoe,
My master's lost his fiddling stick
And knows not what to do.

Cock a doodle doo!
What is my dame to do?
Till master finds his fiddling stick
She'll dance without her shoe.

Cock a doodle doo!
My dame has found her shoe,
And master's found his fiddling stick,
Sing doodle doodle doo.

Cock a doodle doo!
My dame will dance with you,
While master fiddles his fiddling stick
For dame and doodle doo.

GOOSE FEATHERS

Cackle, cackle, Mother Goose,
Have you any feathers loose?
Truly have I, pretty fellow,
Half enough to fill a pillow.
Here are quills, take one or two,
And down to make a bed for you.

DOCTOR FELL

I do not like thee, Doctor Fell,
The reason why I cannot tell;
But this I know, and know full well,
I do not like thee, Doctor Fell.

RACE STARTING

Bell horses, bell horses,
What time of day?
One o'clock, two o'clock,
Three and away.

One to make ready,
And two to prepare;
Good luck to the rider,
And away goes the mare.

One for the money,
Two for the show,
Three to make ready,
And four to go.

RAIN

Rain, rain, go away,
Come again another day,
Little Johnny wants to play.
Rain, rain, go to Spain,
Never show your face again.

BOW-WOW

Bow-wow says the dog,
Mew, mew says the cat,
Grunt, grunt goes the hog,
And squeak goes the rat.

Whoo-oo says the owl,
Caw, caw says the crow,
Quack, quack says the duck,
And what cuckoos say, you know.

So with cuckoos and owls,
With rats and with dogs,
With ducks and with crows,
With cats and with hogs.

A fine song I have made,
To please you, my dear;
And if it's well-sung,
'Twill be charming to hear.

GOING TO ST IVES

As I was going to St Ives,
I met a man with seven wives;
Each wife had seven sacks,
Each sack had seven cats,
Each cat had seven kits:
Kits, cats, sacks, and wives,
How many were there going to St Ives?

HUMPTY DUMPTY

Humpty Dumpty sat on a wall,
Humpty Dumpty had a great fall;
All the King's horses and all the King's men
Couldn't put Humpty together again.

OLD WOMAN

There was an old woman
Lived under a hill,
And if she's not gone
She lives there still.

BABY BUNTING

Bye, baby bunting,
Daddy's gone a-hunting,
Gone to get a rabbit skin
To wrap the baby bunting in.

LUCY AND KITTY

Lucy Locket lost her pocket,
Kitty Fisher found it;
Not a penny was there in it,
Only ribbon round it.

TOM, TOM

Tom, Tom, the piper's son,
Stole a pig and away he run;
The pig was eat, and Tom was beat,
And Tom went roaring down the street.

THE OLD WOMAN WHO
LIVED IN A SHOE

There was an old woman who lived in a shoe;
She had so many children she didn't know what to do.
She gave them some broth without any bread;
Then whipped them all soundly and put them to bed.

THREE BLIND MICE

Three blind mice, see how they run!
They all ran after the farmer's wife,
Who cut off their tails with a carving knife,
Did you ever see such a thing in your life,
    As three blind mice?

IPSEY WIPSEY SPIDER

Ipsey Wipsey spider, climbing up the spout;
Down came the rain and washed the spider out;
Out came the sunshine and dried up all the rain;
Ipsey Wipsey spider, climbing up again.

SOLOMON GRUNDY

Solomon Grundy,
Born on a Monday,
Christened on Tuesday,
Married on Wednesday,
Took ill on Thursday,
Worse on Friday,
Died on Saturday,
Buried on Sunday.
This is the end
Of Solomon Grundy.

A FROG HE WOULD
A-WOOING GO

A frog he would a-wooing go,
Heigh ho! says Rowley,
Whether his mother would let him or no.
With a rowley, powley, gammon and spinach,
Heigh ho! says Anthony Rowley.

So off he set with his opera hat,
Heigh ho! says Rowley,
And on the road he met with a rat.
With a rowley, powley, gammon and spinach,
Heigh ho! says Anthony Rowley.

Pray, Mister Rat, will you go with me?
Heigh ho! says Rowley,
Kind Mrs. Mousey for to see?
With a rowley, powley, gammon and spinach,
Heigh ho! says Anthony Rowley.

They came to the door of Mousey's hall,
Heigh ho! says Rowley,
They gave a loud knock, and they gave a loud call.
With a rowley, powley, gammon and spinach,
Heigh ho! says Anthony Rowley.

Pray, Mrs. Mouse, are you within?
Heigh ho! says Rowley,
Oh yes, kind sirs; I'm sitting to spin.
With a rowley, powley, gammon and spinach,
Heigh ho! says Anthony Rowley.

Pray, Mrs. Mouse, will you give us some beer?
Heigh ho! says Rowley,
For Froggy and I are fond of good cheer.
With a rowley, powley, gammon and spinach,
Heigh ho! says Anthony Rowley.

Pray, Mr. Frog, will you give us a song?
Heigh ho! says Rowley,
Let it be something that's not very long.
With a rowley, powley, gammon and spinach,
Heigh ho! says Anthony Rowley.

Indeed, Mrs. Mouse, replied Mr. Frog,
Heigh ho! says Rowley,
A cold has made me as hoarse as a dog.
With a rowley, powley, gammon and spinach,
Heigh ho! says Anthony Rowley.

Since you have a cold, Mr. Frog, Mousey said,
Heigh ho! says Rowley,
I'll sing you a song that I have just made.
With a rowley, powley, gammon and spinach,
Heigh ho! says Anthony Rowley.

But while they were all a-merry-making,
Heigh ho! says Rowley,
A cat and her kittens came tumbling in.
With a rowley, powley, gammon and spinach,
Heigh ho! says Anthony Rowley.

The cat she seized the rat by the crown,
Heigh ho! says Rowley,
The kittens they pulled the little mouse down.
With a rowley, powley, gammon and spinach,
Heigh ho! says Anthony Rowley.

This put Mr. Frog in a terrible fright,
Heigh ho! says Anthony Rowley,
He took up his hat and he wished them good-night.
With a rowley, powley, gammon and spinach,
Heigh ho! says Anthony Rowley.

But as Froggy was crossing over a brook,
Heigh ho! says Rowley,
A lily-white duck came and gobbled him up.
With a rowley, powley, gammon and spinach,
Heigh ho! says Anthony Rowley.

JACK HORNER

Little Jack Horner
Sat in the corner,
Eating his Christmas pie;
He put in his thumb,
And pulled out a plum,
And said, "What a good boy am I!"

RIDE A COCK-HORSE

Ride a cock-horse to Banbury Cross,
To see a fine lady upon a white horse;
Rings on her fingers and bells on her toes,
She shall have music wherever she goes.

OLD ROGER

Old Roger is dead and laid in his grave,
Laid in his grave, laid in his grave;
Old Roger is dead and laid in his grave,
Hum ha! laid in his grave.

They planted an apple tree over his head,
Over his head, over his head;
They planted an apple tree over his head,
Hum ha! over his head.

The apples grew ripe and ready to fall,
Ready to fall, ready to fall;
The apples grew ripe and ready to fall,
Hum ha! ready to fall.

There came an old woman a-picking them all,
A-picking them all, a-picking them all;
There came an old woman a-picking them all,
Hum ha! picking them all.

Old Roger jumps up and gives her a knock,
Gives her a knock, gives her a knock;
Which makes the old woman go hippety-hop,
Hum ha! hippety-hop.

DIDDLE, DIDDLE, DUMPLING

Diddle, diddle, dumpling, my son John,
Went to bed with his trousers on;
One shoe off, and one shoe on,
Diddle, diddle, dumpling, my son John.

JEREMIAH OBADIAH

Jeremiah Obadiah, puff, puff, puff.
When he gives his messages he snuffs, snuffs, snuffs,
When he goes to school by day, he roars, roars, roars,
When he goes to bed at night he snores, snores, snores.
When he goes to Christmas treat he eats plum-duff,
Jeremiah Obadiah, puff, puff, puff.

AN OLD WOMAN

There was an old woman tossed up in a basket,
Seventeen times as high as the moon;
Where she was going I couldn't but ask it,
For in her hand she carried a broom.

Old woman, old woman, old woman, said I,
Where are you going to up so high?
To brush the cobwebs off the sky!
Shall I go with you? Aye, by-and-by.

THREE YOUNG RATS

Three young rats with black felt hats,
Three young ducks with new straw flats,
Three young dogs with curling tails,
Three young cats with demi-veils,
Went out to walk with two young pigs
In satin vests and sorrel wigs;
But suddenly it chanced to rain
And so they all went home again.

POP GOES THE WEASEL!

Up and down the City Road,
In and out the Eagle,
That's the way the money goes,
Pop goes the weasel!

Half a pound of tuppenny rice,
Half a pound of treacle,
Mix it up and make it nice,
Pop goes the weasel!

Every night when I go out
The monkey's on the table;
Take a stick and knock it off,
Pop goes the weasel!

If you want to buy a pig,
Buy a pig with hairs on,
Every hair a penny a pair,
Pop goes the weasel!

IF ALL THE SEAS

If all the seas were one sea,
What a *great* sea that would be!
If all the trees were one tree,
What a *great* tree that would be!
And if all the axes were one ax,
What a *great* ax that would be!
And if all the men were one man,
What a *great* man he would be!
And if the *great* man took the *great* ax,
And cut down the *great* tree,
And let it fall into the *great* sea,
What a splish-splash that would be!

TOMMY TUCKER

Little Tommy Tucker
Sings for his supper:
What shall we give him?
White bread and butter.
How shall he cut it
Without e'er a knife?
How shall he marry
Without e'er a wife?

THE CAT AND THE FIDDLE

Hey diddle, diddle, the cat and the fiddle,
The cow jumped over the moon;
The little dog laughed to see such sport,
And the dish ran away with the spoon.

CHRISTMAS IS COMING

Christmas is coming,
The geese are getting fat,
Please to put a penny
In the old man's hat.
If you haven't got a penny,
A ha'penny will do;
If you haven't got a ha'penny,
Then God bless you!

GUNPOWDER PLOT

Please to remember
The fifth of November,
Gunpowder treason and plot;
I see no reason
Why gunpowder treason
Should ever be forgot.

PINS

See a pin and pick it up,
All the day you'll have good luck.
See a pin and let it lay,
Bad luck you'll have all the day.

IF WISHES WERE
HORSES

If wishes were horses, beggars would ride.
If turnips were watches, I would
    wear one by my side.
And if "ifs" and "ands" were pots and pans,
There'd be no work for tinkers!

THIS LITTLE PIG WENT TO MARKET

This little pig went to market;
This little pig stayed at home;

This little pig had roast beef;
This little pig had none;
And this little pig cried, Wee-wee-wee,
And ran all the way home.

THE MAD MAN

There was a man, he went mad,

He jumped into a paper bag;

The paper bag was too narrow,

He jumped into a wheelbarrow;

The wheelbarrow took on fire,

He jumped into a cow byre;

The cow byre was too nasty,

He jumped into an apple pasty;

The apple pasty was too sweet,

He jumped into Chester-le-Street;

Chester-le-Street was full of stones,

He fell down and broke his bones.

IF ALL THE WORLD WAS PAPER

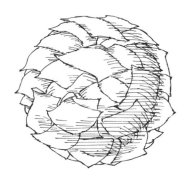

If all the world was paper,

And all the seas were ink,

If all the trees were bread and cheese,

What should we have to drink?

STAR LIGHT

Star light, star bright,
First star I see tonight,
I wish I may, I wish I might,
Have the wish I wish tonight.

PETER WHITE

Peter White will ne'er go right;
Would you know the reason why?
He follows his nose wherever he goes,
And that stands all awry.

PEASE PORRIDGE

Pease porridge hot,
Pease porridge cold,
Pease porridge in the pot,
Nine days old.
Some like it hot,
Some like it cold,
Some like it in the pot,
Nine days old.

GOOSEY GANDER

Goosey, goosey gander,
Whither shall I wander?
Upstairs and downstairs
And in my lady's chamber.
There I met an old man
Who wouldn't say his prayers,
I took him by the left leg
And threw him down the stairs.

POLLY PUT THE KETTLE ON

Polly put the kettle on,
Polly put the kettle on,
Polly put the kettle on,
We'll all have tea.

Sukey take it off again,
Sukey take it off again,
Sukey take it off again,
They've all gone away.

THREE LITTLE KITTENS

Three little kittens
They lost their mittens,
And they began to cry,
Oh, Mother dear,
We sadly fear
Our mittens we have lost.
What! lost your mittens,
You naughty kittens!
Then you shall have no pie.
Mee-ow, mee-ow, mee-ow.
No, you shall have no pie.

The three little kittens
They found their mittens,
And they began to cry,
Oh, Mother dear,
See here, see here,
For we have found our mittens.
Put on your mittens,
You silly kittens,
And you shall have some pie.
Purr-r, purr-r, purr-r,
Oh, let us have some pie.

The three little kittens
Put on their mittens
And soon ate up the pie;
Oh, Mother dear,
We greatly fear
That we have soiled our mittens.
What! soiled your mittens,
You naughty kittens!
Then they began to sigh,
Mee-ow, mee-ow, mee-ow,
Then they began to sigh.

The three little kittens
They washed their mittens,
And hung them out to dry;
Oh, Mother dear,
Do you not hear,
That we have washed our mittens.
What! washed your mittens,
Then you're good kittens,
But I smell a rat close by.
Mee-ow, mee-ow, mee-ow,
We smell a rat close by.

JEREMIAH

Jeremiah, blow the fire,
Puff, puff, puff!
First you blow it gently,
Then you blow it rough.

ANNA MARIA

Anna Maria, she sat on the fire;
The fire was too hot, she sat on the pot;
The pot was too round, she sat on the ground;
The ground was too flat, she sat on the cat;
The cat ran away with Maria on her back.

OLD MOTHER SHUTTLE

Old Mother Shuttle,
Lived in a coal-scuttle
Along with her dog and her cat;
What they ate I can't tell,
But 'tis known very well
That none of the party was fat.

Old Mother Shuttle
Scoured out her coal-scuttle,
And washed both her dog and her cat;
The cat scratched her nose,
So they came to hard blows,
And who was the gainer by that?

83

SING A SONG OF SIXPENCE

Sing a song of sixpence,
A pocket full of rye;
Four-and-twenty blackbirds,
Baked in a pie.

When the pie was opened,
The birds began to sing;
Was not that a dainty dish,
To set before the king?

THE WISE MEN OF GOTHAM

Three wise men of Gotham
Went to sea in a bowl.
If the bowl had been stronger,
My song had been longer.

The king was in his counting-house,
Counting out his money;
The queen was in the parlor
Eating bread and honey.

The maid was in the garden,
Hanging out the clothes,
When down came a blackbird
And pecked off her nose.

THE SOLDIER AND THE MAID

Oh, soldier, soldier, will you marry me,
With your musket, fife, and drum?
Oh no, pretty maid, I cannot marry you,
For I have no coat to put on.

Then off she went to the tailor's shop
As fast as legs could run,
And bought him one of the very very best,
And the soldier put it on.

Oh, soldier, soldier, will you marry me,
With your musket, fife, and drum?
Oh no, pretty maid, I cannot marry you,
For I have no shoes to put on.

Then off she went to the cobbler's shop
As fast as legs could run,
And bought him a pair of the very very best,
And the soldier put them on.

Oh, soldier, soldier, will you marry me,
With your musket, fife, and drum?
Oh no, pretty maid, I cannot marry you,
For I have no socks to put on.

Then off she went to the sock-maker's shop
As fast as legs could run,
And bought him a pair of the very very best,
And the soldier put them on.

Oh, soldier, soldier, will you marry me,
With your musket, fife, and drum?
Oh no, pretty maid, I cannot marry you,
For I have no hat to put on.

Then off she went to the hatter's shop
As fast as legs could run,
And bought him one of the very very best,
And the soldier put it on.

Oh, soldier, soldier, will you marry me,
With your musket, fife, and drum?
Oh no, pretty maid, I cannot marry you,
For I have a wife of my own.

THE QUEEN OF HEARTS

The Queen of Hearts
She made some tarts,
All on a summer's day;
The Knave of Hearts
He stole the tarts,
And took them clean away.

The King of Hearts
Called for the tarts,
And beat the knave full sore;
The Knave of Hearts
Brought back the tarts,
And vowed he'd steal no more.

PUSSY-CAT

Pussy-cat, pussy-cat,
Where have you been?
I've been to London
To look at the Queen.
Pussy-cat, pussy-cat,
What did you there?
I frightened a little mouse
Under her chair.

THE MISCHIEVOUS RAVEN

A farmer went trotting upon his gray mare,
Bumpety, bumpety, bump!
With his daughter behind him so rosy and fair,
Lumpety, lumpety, lump!

A raven cried, Croak! and they all tumbled down,
Bumpety, bumpety, bump!
The mare broke her knees and the farmer his crown,
Lumpety, lumpety, lump!

The mischievous raven flew laughing away,
Bumpety, bumpety, bump!
And vowed he would serve them the same the next day,
Lumpety, lumpety, lump!

HANNAH BANTRY

Hannah Bantry,
In the pantry,
Gnawing at a mutton bone;
How she gnawed it,
How she clawed it,
When she found herself alone.

THE BAT

Bat, bat, come under my hat,
And I'll give you a slice of bacon;
And when I bake, I'll give you a cake,
If I am not mistaken.

TWEEDLEDUM AND TWEEDLEDEE

Tweedledum and Tweedledee
Agreed to have a battle,
For Tweedledum said Tweedledee
Had spoiled his nice new rattle.
Just then flew by a monstrous crow
As big as a tar-barrel,
Which frightened both the heroes so,
They quite forgot their quarrel.

THE GIANT

Fee, fi, fo, fum!
I smell the blood of an Englishman.
Be he alive or be he dead,
I'll grind his bones to make my bread.

THREE GHOSTESSES

Three little ghostesses,
Sitting on postesses,
Eating buttered toastesses,
Greasing their fistesses,
Up to their wristesses.
Oh, what beastesses
To make such feastesses!

IF I HAD A DONKEY

If I had a donkey that wouldn't go,
Would I beat him? Oh no, no.
I'd put him in the barn and give him some corn.
The best little donkey that ever was born.

THE JOLLY MILLER

There was a jolly miller once,
Lived on the river Dee;
He worked and sang from morn till night,
No lark more blithe than he.
And this the burden of his song
Forever used to be,
I care for nobody, no, not I,
If nobody cares for me.

JACK-A-NORY

I'll tell you a story
About Jack-a-Nory,
And now my story's begun;
I'll tell you another
About his brother,
And now my story is done.

A RAT

There was a rat, for want of stairs,
Went down a rope to say his prayers.

GIRLS AND BOYS COME OUT TO PLAY

Girls and boys come out to play,
The moon doth shine as bright as day.
Leave your supper and leave your sleep,
And come with your playfellows into the street.
Come with a whoop and come with a call,
Come with a good will or not at all.
Up the ladder and down the wall,
A half-penny loaf will serve us all;
You find milk, and I'll find flour,
And we'll have a pudding in half an hour.

GEORGIE PORGIE

Georgie Porgie, pudding and pie,
Kissed the girls and made them cry.
When the boys came out to play,
Georgie Porgie ran away.

A MAN OF THESSALY

There was a man of Thessaly
And he was wondrous wise,
He jumped into a bramble bush
And scratched out both his eyes.
And when he saw his eyes were out,
With all his might and main
He jumped into another bush
And scratched them in again.

TWINKLE, TWINKLE

Twinkle, twinkle, little star,
How I wonder what you are!
Up above the world so high,
Like a diamond in the sky.

THE LITTLE NUT TREE

I had a little nut tree,
Nothing would it bear
But a silver nutmeg
And a golden pear.
The king of Spain's daughter
Came to visit me,
All for the sake
Of my little nut tree.

SIX LITTLE MICE

Six little mice sat down to spin;
Pussy passed by and she peeped in.
What are you doing, my little men?
Weaving coats for gentlemen.
Shall I come in and cut off your threads?
No, no, Mistress Pussy, you'd bite off our heads.
Oh, no, I'll not; I'll help you to spin.
That may be so, but you don't come in.

QUEEN CAROLINE

Queen, Queen Caroline,
Washed her hair in turpentine,
Turpentine to make it shine,
Queen, Queen Caroline.

LITTLE BOY BLUE

Little Boy Blue,
Come blow your horn.
The sheep's in the meadow,
The cow's in the corn.
Where is the boy
That looks after the sheep?
He's under a haystack
Fast asleep.
Will you wake him?
No, not I,
For if I do,
He's sure to cry.

BAA, BAA, BLACK SHEEP

Baa, baa, black sheep,
Have you any wool?
Yes, sir, yes, sir,
Three bags full;
One for the master,
And one for the dame,
And one for the little boy
Who lives down the lane.

THE HOUSE THAT JACK BUILT

This is the house
 that Jack built.

This is the malt
That lay in the house
 that Jack built.

This is the rat,
That ate the malt
That lay in the house
 that Jack built.

This is the cat,
That killed the rat,
That ate the malt
That lay in the house
  that Jack built.

This is the dog,
That worried the cat,
That killed the rat,
That ate the malt
That lay in the house
  that Jack built.

This is the cow
   with the crumpled horn,
That tossed the dog,
That worried the cat,
That killed the rat,
That ate the malt
That lay in the house
   that Jack built.

This is the maiden all forlorn,
That milked the cow
   with the crumpled horn,
That tossed the dog,
That worried the cat,
That killed the rat,
That ate the malt
That lay in the house
   that Jack built.

This is the man all tattered and torn,
That kissed the maiden all forlorn,
That milked the cow
   with the crumpled horn,
That tossed the dog,
That worried the cat,
That killed the rat,
That ate the malt
That lay in the house
    that Jack built.

This is the priest all shaven and shorn,
That married the man
   all tattered and torn,
That kissed the maiden all forlorn,
That milked the cow
   with the crumpled horn,
That tossed the dog,
That worried the cat,
That killed the rat,
That ate the malt
That lay in the house
    that Jack built.

This is the cock
   that crowed in the morn,
That waked the priest
   all shaven and shorn,
That married the man
   all tattered and torn,
That kissed the maiden
   all forlorn,
That milked the cow
   with the crumpled horn,
That tossed the dog,
That worried the cat,
That killed the rat,
That ate the malt
That lay in the house
   that Jack built.

This is the farmer sowing his corn,
That kept the cock that crowed in the morn,
That waked the priest all shaven and shorn,
That married the man all tattered and torn,
That kissed the maiden all forlorn,
That milked the cow with the crumpled horn,
That tossed the dog,
That worried the cat,
That killed the rat,
That ate the malt
That lay in the house
    that Jack built.

This is the horse and the hound and the horn,
That belonged to the farmer sowing his corn,
That kept the cock that crowed in the morn,
That waked the priest all shaven and shorn,
That married the man all tattered and torn,
That kissed the maiden all forlorn,
That milked the cow with the crumpled horn,
                    That tossed the dog,
                    That worried the cat,
                    That killed the rat,
                    That ate the malt
                    That lay in the house
                        that Jack built.

TO BABYLON

How many miles to Babylon?
Three-score miles and ten.
Can I get there by candle-light?
Yes, and back again.
If your heels are nimble and light,
You may get there by candle-light.

LAVENDER'S BLUE

Lavender's blue, dilly, dilly,
  lavender's green;
When I am King, dilly, dilly,
  you shall be Queen;
Call up your men, dilly, dilly,
  set them to work:
Some to the plow, dilly, dilly,
  some to the cart,
Some to make hay, dilly, dilly,
  some to thresh corn;
Whilst you and I, dilly, dilly,
  keep ourselves warm.

HECTOR PROTECTOR

Hector Protector was dressed all in green;
Hector Protector was sent to the Queen.
The Queen did not like him;
No more did the King;
So Hector Protector was sent back again.

THE LADYBIRD

Ladybird, ladybird,
Fly away home,
Your house is on fire
Your children all gone;
All but one,
And her name is Ann,
And she has crept under
The warming pan.

THE BELLS OF LONDON

Oranges and lemons,
Say the bells of St Clement's.

You owe me five farthings,
Say the bells of St Martin's.

When will you pay me?
Say the bells of Old Bailey.

When I grow rich,
Say the bells of Shoreditch.

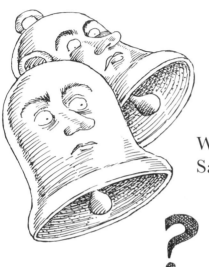

When will that be?
Say the bells of Stepney.

I'm sure I don't know,
Says the Great Bell of Bow.

JACK

Jack be nimble,
Jack be quick,
Jack jump over
The candlestick.

THE GRAND OLD DUKE
OF YORK

Oh, the grand old Duke of York,
He had ten thousand men;
He marched them up to the top of the hill,
And he marched them down again.
And when they were up, they were up,
And when they were down, they were down,
And when they were only half-way up,
They were neither up nor down.

ON SATURDAY NIGHT

On Saturday night I lost my wife,
And where do you think I found her?
Up in the moon, singing a tune,
And all the stars around her.

PUSSY CAT MEW

Pussy cat mew jumped over a coal,
And in her best petticoat burned a great hole;
Pussy cat mew shall have no more milk,
Until her best petticoat's mended with silk.

THE DAYS
OF THE MONTHS

Thirty days hath September,
April, June, and November;
All the rest have thirty-one.
Excepting February alone,
And that has twenty-eight days clear
And twenty-nine in each leap year.

JERRY HALL

Jerry Hall, he is so small,
A rat could eat him, hat and all.

TERENCE
McDIDDLER

Terence McDiddler,
The three-stringed fiddler,
Can charm, if you please,
The fish from the seas.

ALL WORK AND NO PLAY

All work and no play makes Jack a dull boy;
All play and no work makes Jack a mere toy.

A NAIL

For want of a nail the shoe was lost,
For want of a shoe the horse was lost,
For want of a horse the rider was lost,
For want of a rider the battle was lost,
For want of a battle the kingdom was lost,
And all for the want of a horseshoe nail.

TO BED

To bed, to bed,
Says Sleepy-head;
Tarry a while, says Slow;
Put on the pan,
Says Greedy Nan,
We'll sup before we go.

SNAIL, SNAIL

Snail, snail, put out your horns,
And I'll give you bread and barley corns.

HIGGLETY, PIGGLETY

Higglety, pigglety, pop!
The dog has eaten the mop;
The pig's in a hurry,
The cat's in a flurry,
Higglety, pigglety, pop!

ALPHABET PIE

A was an
Apple pie

B
Bit it

C
Cut it

D
Dealt it

E
Eat it

F
Fought for it

G
Got it

H
Had it

I
Inspected it

J
Jumped for it

K
Kept it

L
Longed for it

M
Mourned for it

N
Nodded at it

O
Opened it

P
Peeped in it

Q
Quartered it

R
Ran for it

S
Stole it

T
Took it

U
Upset it

V
Viewed it

W
Wanted it

XYZ and ampersand
All wished for
a piece in hand

COCK ROBIN

Who killed Cock Robin?
I, said the Sparrow,
With my bow and arrow,
I killed Cock Robin.

Who saw him die?
I, said the Fly,
With my little eye,
I saw him die.

Who caught his blood?
I, said the Fish,
With my little dish,
I caught his blood.

Who'll make his shroud?
I, said the Beetle,
With my thread and needle,
I'll make the shroud.

Who'll dig his grave?
I, said the Owl,
With my pick and shovel,
I'll dig his grave.

Who'll be the parson?
I, said the Rook,
With my little book,
I'll be the parson.

Who'll be the clerk?
I, said the Lark,
If it's not in the dark,
I'll be the clerk.

Who'll carry the link?
I, said the Linnet,
I'll fetch it in a minute,
I'll carry the link.

Who'll be chief mourner?
I, said the Dove,
I mourn for my love,
I'll be chief mourner.

Who'll carry the coffin?
I, said the Kite,
If it's not through the night
I'll carry the coffin.

Who'll bear the pall?
We, said the Wren,
Both the cock and the hen,
We'll bear the pall.

Who'll sing a psalm?
I, said the Thrush,
As she sat on a bush,
I'll sing a psalm.

Who'll toll the bell?
I, said the Bull,
Because I can pull,
I'll toll the bell.

All the birds of the air
Fell a-sighing and a-sobbing,
When they heard the bell toll
For poor Cock Robin.

ROBIN THE BOBBIN

Robin the Bobbin, the big-bellied Ben,
He ate more meat than fourscore men;
He ate a cow, he ate a calf,
He ate a butcher and a half,
He ate a church, he ate a steeple,
He ate a priest and all the people!
A cow and a calf,
An ox and a half,
A church and a steeple,
And all the good people,
And yet he complained that his stomach wasn't full.

LITTLE JUMPING JOAN

Here am I,
Little Jumping Joan;
When nobody's with me
I'm always alone.

MOSES

Moses supposes his toeses are roses,
But Moses supposes erroneously;
For nobody's toeses are posies of roses
As Moses supposes his toeses to be.

GREGORY GRIGGS

Gregory Griggs, Gregory Griggs,
Had twenty-seven different wigs.
He wore them up, he wore them down,
To please the people of the town;
He wore them east, he wore them west,
But he never could tell which he loved the best.

KING ARTHUR

When good King Arthur ruled this land,
He was a goodly King;
He stole three pecks of barley-meal
To make a bag-pudding.

A bag-pudding the King did make,
And stuffed it well with plums,
And in it put great lumps of fat,
As big as my two thumbs.

The King and Queen did eat thereof,
And noblemen beside;
And what they could not eat that night,
The Queen next morning fried.

DAVY DUMPLING

Davy Davy Dumpling,
Boil him in the pot;
Sugar him and butter him,
And eat him while he's hot.

THE KEY OF THE KINGDOM

This is the key of the kingdom.
In that kingdom is a city,
In the city is a town,
In that town there is a street,
In that street there winds a lane,
In that lane there is a yard,
In that yard there is a house,
In the house there waits a room,
In that room there is a bed,
On that bed there is a basket,
A basket of flowers.

Flowers in the basket,
Basket on the bed,
Bed in the chamber,
Chamber in the house,
House in the weedy yard,
Yard in the winding lane,
Lane in the broad street,
Street in the high town,
Town in the city,
City in the kingdom:
This is the key of the kingdom.

MARY, MARY

Mary, Mary, quite contrary,
How does your garden grow?
With silver bells and cockle shells,
And pretty maids all in a row.

MY BLACK HEN

Hickety, pickety, my black hen,
She lays eggs for gentlemen;
Gentlemen come every day
To see what my black hen doth lay.

128

ROSES
ARE RED

Roses are red,
Violets are blue,
Sugar is sweet
And so are you.

IT'S RAINING

It's raining, it's pouring,
The old man's snoring;
He got into bed
And bumped his head
And couldn't get up in the morning.

JINGLE BELLS

Jingle, bells! jingle, bells!
Jingle all the way;
Oh, what fun it is to ride
In a one-horse open sleigh.

HOT CROSS BUNS

Hot cross buns! hot cross buns!
One a penny, two a penny,
Hot cross buns!
If you have no daughters
Give them to your sons;
One a penny, two a penny
Hot cross buns.

WHERE, OH WHERE

Oh where, oh where has my little dog gone?
Oh where, oh where can he be?
With his ears cut short and his tail cut long,
Oh where, oh where is he?

SULKY SUE

Here's Sulky Sue;
What shall we do?
Turn her face to the wall
Till she comes to.

THE CROOKED MAN

There was a crooked man,
And he walked a crooked mile,
He found a crooked sixpence
Against a crooked stile;
He bought a crooked cat,
Which caught a crooked mouse,
And they all lived together
In a little crooked house.

THE MILKMAN

Milkman, Milkman, where have you been?
In Buttermilk Channel up to my chin;
I spilt my milk, and I spoilt my clothes,
And got a long icicle hung from my nose.

THE SKY

Red sky at night,
Shepherd's delight;
Red sky in the morning,
Shepherd's warning.

YANKEE DOODLE

Yankee Doodle came to town,
Riding on a pony;
He stuck a feather in his cap
And called it macaroni.

THE KILKENNY CATS

There were once two cats of Kilkenny.
Each thought there was one cat too many;
So they fought and they fit,
And they scratched and they bit,
Till, excepting their nails,
And the tips of their tails,
Instead of two cats, there weren't any.

A MAN IN THE WILDERNESS

A man in the wilderness said to me,
How many strawberries grow in the sea?
I answered him, as I thought good,
As many red herrings as grow in the wood.

THE MAN WITH NOUGHT

There was a man and he had nought,
And robbers came to rob him;
He crept up to the chimney pot,
And then they thought they had him.

But he got down on the other side,
And then they could not find him;
He ran fourteen miles in fifteen days,
And never looked behind him.

THE MAGPIE

Magpie, magpie, flutter and flee,
Turn up your tail and good luck come to me.
One for sorrow, two for joy,
Three for a girl, four for a boy,
Five for silver, six for gold,
Seven for a secret ne'er to be told.

THE MILK MAID

Where are you going to, my pretty maid?
I'm going a-milking, sir, she said,
Sir, she said, sir, she said,
I'm going a-milking, sir, she said.

May I go with you, my pretty maid?
You're kindly welcome, sir, she said,
Sir, she said, sir, she said,
You're kindly welcome, sir, she said.

Say, will you marry me, my pretty maid?
Yes, if you please, kind sir, she said,
Sir, she said, sir, she said,
Yes, if you please, kind sir, she said.

What is your father, my pretty maid?
My father's a farmer, sir, she said,
Sir, she said, sir, she said,
My father's a farmer, sir, she said.

What is your fortune, my pretty maid?
My face is my fortune, sir, she said,
Sir, she said, sir, she said,
My face is my fortune, sir, she said.

Then I can't marry you, my pretty maid.
Nobody asked you, sir, she said,
Sir, she said, sir, she said,
Nobody asked you, sir, she said.

CORPORAL BULL

Here's Corporal Bull
A strong hearty fellow,
Who not used to fighting
Set up a loud bellow.

THE CUCKOO

Cuckoo, cuckoo, what do you do?
In April I open my bill;
In May I sing all day;
In June I change my tune;
In July away I fly;
In August away I must.

THE WIND

When the wind is in the east,
'Tis neither good for man nor beast;
When the wind is in the north,
The skillful fisher goes not forth;
When the wind is in the south,
It blows the bait in the fishes' mouth;
When the wind is in the west,
Then 'tis at the very best.

TEN O'CLOCK SCHOLAR

A diller, a dollar,
A ten o'clock scholar,
What makes you come so soon?
You used to come at ten o'clock,
But now you come at noon.

THE LITTLE MAN

There was a little man, and he had a little gun
And his bullets were made of lead, lead, lead;
He went to the brook, and saw a little duck,
And shot it through the head, head, head.

He carried it home to his old wife Joan,
And bade her a fire to make, make, make;
To roast the little duck, while he went to the brook,
To shoot and kill the drake, drake, drake.

THE PIE

Who made the pie?
I did.
Who stole the pie?
He did.
Who found the pie?
She did.
Who ate the pie?
You did.
Who cried for pie?
We all did.

HUSH, LITTLE BABY

Hush, little baby, don't say a word,
Papa's going to buy you a mocking bird.

If the mocking bird won't sing,
Papa's going to buy you a diamond ring.

If the diamond ring turns to brass,
Papa's going to buy you a looking-glass.

If the looking-glass gets broke,
Papa's going to buy you a billy goat.

If that billy goat runs away,
Papa's going to buy you another today.

THE FLYING PIG

Dickery, dickery, dare,
The pig flew up in the air;
The man in brown
Soon brought him down,
Dickery, dickery, dare.

SEE-SAW, MARGERY DAW

See-saw, Margery Daw,
Jacky shall have a new master;
Jacky shall have but a penny a day,
Because he can't work any faster.

THE BEGGARS

Hark, hark, the dogs do bark,
The beggars are coming to town;
Some in jags and some in rags,
And one in a velvet gown.

MY FATHER DIED

My father died a month ago
And left me all his riches;
A feather bed, a wooden leg,
And a pair of leather breeches;
A coffee pot without a spout,
A cup without a handle,
A tobacco pipe without a lid,
And half a farthing candle.

A WEEK OF BIRTHDAYS

Monday's child is fair of face,
Tuesday's child is full of grace,
Wednesday's child is full of woe,
Thursday's child has far to go,
Friday's child is loving and giving,
Saturday's child works hard for its living,
But the child that's born on the Sabbath day
Is bonny and blithe, and good and gay.

I SAW A SHIP A-SAILING

I saw a ship a-sailing,
A-sailing on the sea,
And oh, but it was laden
With pretty things for thee!

There were comfits in the cabin,
And apples in the hold;
The sails were made of silk,
And the masts were made of gold.

The four-and-twenty sailors,
That stood between the decks,
Were four-and-twenty white mice
With chains about their necks.

The captain was a duck
With a packet on his back,
And when the ship began to move
The captain said, Quack! Quack!

BANDY LEGS

As I was going to sell my eggs
I met a man with bandy legs,
Bandy legs and crooked toes;
I tripped up his heels, and he fell on his nose.

LITTLE TOMMY TITTLEMOUSE

Little Tommy Tittlemouse
Lived in a little house;
He caught fishes
In other men's ditches.

HODDLEY, PODDLEY

Hoddley, poddley, puddle and fogs,
Cats are to marry the poodle dogs;
Cats in blue jackets and dogs in red hats,
What will become of the mice and the rats?

THE MULBERRY BUSH

Here we go round the mulberry bush,
The mulberry bush, the mulberry bush,
Here we go round the mulberry bush,
On a cold and frosty morning.

This is the way we wash our hands,
Wash our hands, wash our hands,
This is the way we wash our hands,
On a cold and frosty morning.

This is the way we wash our clothes,
Wash our clothes, wash our clothes,
This is the way we wash our clothes,
On a cold and frosty morning.

This is the way we go to school,
Go to school, go to school,
This is the way we go to school,
On a cold and frosty morning.

This is the way we come out of school,
Come out of school, come out of school,
This is the way we come out of school,
On a cold and frosty morning.

HICKORY,
DICKORY,
DOCK

Hickory, dickory, dock,
The mouse ran up the clock.
The clock struck one,
The mouse ran down,
Hickory, dickory, dock.

ONE, TWO, THREE, FOUR, FIVE

One, two three, four, five,
Once I caught a fish alive,
Six, seven, eight, nine, ten,
Then I let it go again.
Why did you let it go?
Because it bit my finger so.
Which finger did it bite?
This little finger on the right.

BEDTIME

The Man in the Moon
  looked out of the moon,
Looked out of the moon and said,
"'Tis time for all children on the earth
To think about getting to bed!"

THE MOON

I see the moon,
And the moon sees me;
God bless the moon,
And God bless me.

A PRAYER

Now I lay me down to sleep,
I pray the Lord my soul to keep;
And if I die before I wake,
I pray the Lord my soul to take.

Index of First Lines